Copyright © 2022 by Mrs Helen Miller

All rights reserved. This book or any portion thereof may not be reproduced or used in any manner whatsoever without the express written permission of the publisher except for the use of brief quotations in a book review.
Printed in the United States of America
First Printing, 2021
ISBN 9798419426450
Winter Fall Publishing
171 Gilbert Street
Columbus, OH 43206

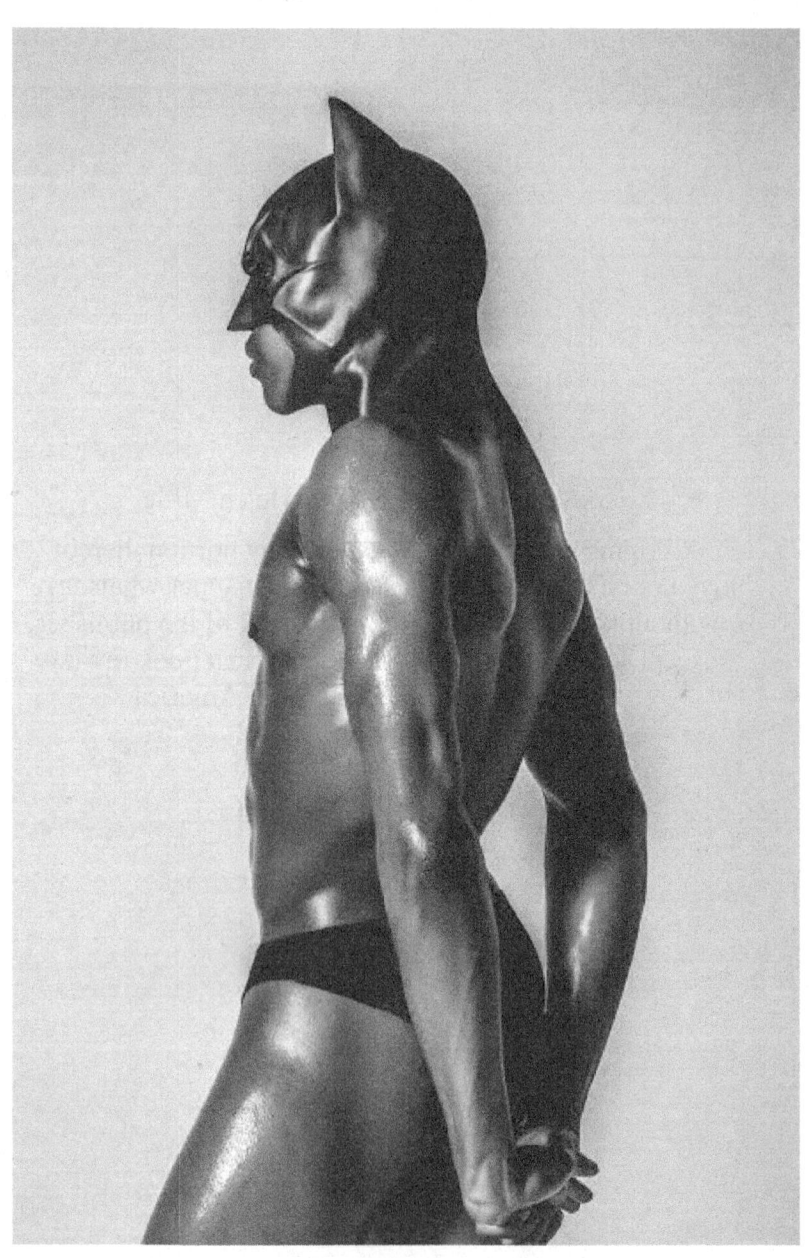

INTRODUCTION: 4
CHAPTER 1 5
CHAPTER 2 14
CHAPTER 3 22
CHAPTER 4 29
CHAPTER 5 37
CHAPTER 6 46
CHAPTER 7 50
CHAPTER 8 54
CHAPTER 9 64
CHAPTER 10 68
CHAPTER 11 78
CHAPTER 12 88
CHAPTER 13 100
CHAPTER 14 108
CHAPTER 15 112
CHAPTER 16 116
CHAPTER 17 123

INTRODUCTION:
BATMAN SHOWS HIS PROMISCIOUS SIDE

I was a big fan of the Batman series starring Adam West as a campy Batman in the 1960's. I always wondered what Batman did for sex. Now I know. I know it's stupid and goofy—that's the way I wrote it. I hope you enjoy reading it and please leave me a positive review. Thank you

CHAPTER 1

Bruce wayne was quite satisfied with himself as he stood in the study of stately wayne manor. Not only was crime in Gotham City down 40 percent thanks to his superhero alter ego Batman, but he had just completed his latest invention—the Invisibility Cloaking Device (ICD)—and installed it at last on the Batmobile. The clock in the hallway struck three o'clock, time for his daily appointment with his shapely secretary Stephanie. A lot of people thought that Batman had a dark side—and they were right! Bruce often admitted to himself that he was a fucking pervert, to whom nothing was out-of-bounds.

Just then Stephanie walked into the room. She lowered her head to her ample chest. "I'm sorry I'm late, sir—uh, I mean Master." As she knelt before the Batman in his secret identity she knew that he would have to punish her, just what she wanted. She looked at the nearby switch yearning for its sting across her firm buttocks.

"Why were you late, Slave?" Bruce asked, a sneer crossing his handsome face.

"I had to go to my room, Master. I had to remove my panties."

"What?!! Why were you wearing panties in direct violation of my orders? Yes, you are definitely going to be punished."

"Yes, Master, I deserve to be punished. I had to go to the super market so I dressed for outside, but when I returned I forgot to remove them...Master. Please punish me. I deserve it."

With that Bruce pulled her up, led her to the big leather chair, and placed her across his knees. Stephanie had worked for him for more than two years, ever since she had graduated from college—the Gotham Institute of Technology, also commonly known to locals as the Gotham Institute of Slutology, because of all the sex maniac girls who attended. When Bruce had checked Stephanie's resume and application his status as the university's greatest benefactor opened many doors. He learned that she had slept her way to passing grades in almost every

class, passing only Phys. Ed. on her own merits. Nonetheless, Bruce had hired her, and at a high salary for such a position, knowing that some day he would take great advantage of her sexuality. From the onset Stephanie had been submissive, almost begging for the opportunity to serve Bruce, but he had tortured her by sticking to business for well over a year. One day he had just come out and told her to remove her panties and to never wear them in the house again. Once she recovered from the shock, he could see the expression of desire on her face as she pushed the plain white cotton undies down over her ankles. Bruce then told her to bend over the arm of the big leather upholstered chair in the study. She had looked at him questioningly, but her natural tendencies toward submissiveness led her to follow his directive.

"From now on you will come here every day at three o'clock. Do you understand me?"

"Yes, sir," she barely whispered, her well-trimmed pussy already gushing hot juice.

"At that time every day you will service me with your mouth, pussy, and ass. I want to be able to smell your excitement. That is why I do not want you to wear any panties. Do you understand me now?

"Yes, sir."

"Explain to me what you will do. Explain in detail. I want to hear you say it."

"I will come here ever afternoon at three o'clock to service you with my mouth, my pussy, and my ass. I will suck your cock if you wish and let you fuck my pussy and ass."

"Is this something you want to do for me," the Batman/Bruce asked.

"Oh, yes, sir. I want to serve...I mean service you. I want to do it very much."

"Very good then; you are to be my slave. You will do everything I ask. You will not refuse me anything no matter how depraved or filthy you may think it to be. You are not to have an orgasm without my permission. That will only make you more eager to suck and fuck me. When you are good I will reward you with orgasms and presents; when you are bad, I will punish you. Understand? Agree?"

"Yes, Master. I will gladly be your slave. I will do whatever you wish me to do."

Then Bruce stepped up behind her, dropped his pants and slid his huge cock into her already soaking wet pussy. Stephanie groaned with pleasure at the sensation of his mammoth erection filling her. Bruce had never actually measured his cock, but he knew that he was much bigger than any of his friends—

MUCH BIGGER. Had he bothered, he would have learned that he was almost twelve inches in length and almost three inches in diameter. Batman was hung like a fucking horse! It wasn't always that way. All throughout school Bruce had been subjected to the taunts and jeers of his classmates because of his tiny dick. It wasn't until he decided to study abroad during his junior year of college that this changed. His studies brought him to Tibet where he traveled extensively. One night in search of lodging he stumbled onto a monastery. He was given food and a cell, as the monks called their small sparsely furnished rooms. In the morning he went to urinate with the monks in the slit trench that had been built for that purpose. All the monks, the Monks of the Ancient Order, had huge thick cocks. They couldn't help but notice his dinky two-incher. Later that morning Bruce was summoned to the office of the Lama.

"Come in, my son," said the Lama in nearly perfect English. "Do you know why I have summoned you?"

"No, Lama," Bruce responded. "But I am curious about something. At the trench this morning I noticed that all of the monks have very large penises. How can that be?"

"That is why I have called for you. Have you been embarrassed by the size of your member? Have you been teased by your friends and classmates?"

"Yes, Lama, it has been the source of much pain for me," said Bruce softly, his head on his chest.

"Many have come here for the same reason. We have a secret treatment, a gift from the Ancients that will grow your penis just as we have grown those of the monks. But I am hesitant to give it to you. It will cause your penis to grow as if by magic, but there is also a curse involved. That is why so many have

decided to return here to the monastery and live as monks."

"What is the curse, Lama?" Bruce inquired.

"Whenever a woman sees or touches your organ she will have an uncontrollable urge to mate with you. That may seem a blessing, but many have found it is not. That is the curse. Do you wish to submit to the treatment?"

Bruce thought for a moment-- Hmm. I'd have a huge cock that girls would die over.--where's the curse in that? "Yes," he replied, "I wish to submit to the treatment."

"Very well, we will start tomorrow morning. Get a good night's rest. You will need it in the morning. You may go now."

The following morning Bruce started the arduous treatment. It was extremely difficult, but three days later a huge change had occurred. His dinky penis, only two inches soft, had grown to seven. His erection, once only four and a half inches, was now almost twelve. He stayed with the monks for another week to regain his strength after the ordeal he had experienced. Then he left and flew home eager to try his new cock.

CHAPTER 2

Bruce had fucked her hard for several minutes observing how rapidly she lost control of her body, how quickly she succumbed to the wanton desire within her. No wonder she had gotten such good grades in college. When he thought she was ready, Bruce rammed a finger into her ass. She almost screamed, but somehow she knew a good slave wouldn't. It wasn't as though she had never had a date, or a professor, stick anything up there. Her Sociolology instructor was strictly an ass man—he never touched her pussy. Over time she had learned to have thunderous orgasms from anal sex. Suddenly, Bruce had removed his slimy cock from her tunnel and shoved it into her hot ass. She screamed initially from the pain and later from the ecstasy. "Thank you,

Master," she had said, "I really needed that." After Bruce had opened her sphincter it only took a few minutes for him to cum, followed only a few seconds later by her lengthy climax. Then he sat in the chair and told his slave to lick his cock clean. Stephanie had never done anything like that before but she wanted to please her new master, so tentatively she started to lick the hard monster clean. She could easily discern her own ass juices from the taste of his cum. She'd tasted plenty of cum during the past nine years since she had started to have sex when only sixteen. In fact, she and several of her high school friends had formed a blowjob club. To get in a girl had to have a photo of her partner blowing his seed in her mouth. There had been plenty of members, and more applications every day.

That's how it had all started almost six months ago; Stephanie had never been happier. She was even more elated when Bruce told her to move into stately Wayne Manor so she could service him at any time of day or night. But, today she had to be punished. She

hadn't forgotten to take off the panties. She wanted, no, she craved the punishment. She loved the feeling of Bruce's strong hand, or the switch, smacking into her firm buttocks. When Bruce sat into the chair—their chair, the site of so many of their sexual encounters—she slowly lay across his knees. Bruce raised her skirt, admiring her tight round ass, massaging it as a prelude to the punishment. At five foot nine, 125 pounds, she really had a fantastic body—large globes for breasts with the longest nipples he had ever seen, a round muscular ass, and flat abs leading to a prominent mound-- and it was all his. He raised his hand and brought it down forcefully. Smack! "One," she counted. Again, another smack; again she counted, tears starting to form in her eyes. And so it went for three more spanks when suddenly the Batphone rang.

Stephanie knew of his work as Batman, of course. All the servants, under the supervision of the ever-present Alfred, knew and were sworn to secrecy, in return for life-long employment. Quickly, Bruce rose

and strode to the phone. "Yes, Commissioner Gordon, Batman here," he spoke into the receiver.

"Batman, we have an emergency. A group of gunmen has broken into the Gotham Federal Bank. We know they have some hostages from those that escaped. We need your help, Caped Crusader, and we need it now!"

"I'll be right there, Commissioner." By the time he hung up the Batphone Stephanie had opened the secret panel revealing the Bat Poles which led,of course, to the subterranean caverns known to all as the Bat Cave, the headquarters for the Dynamic Duo. "We'll continue this when I return," he said before kissing her briefly and descending thru the auto-clothes changer, another of his inventions. Unfortunately, his ward Dick Grayson, Robin in his crime fighting guise, was in school at this hour so he'd have to handle this one alone. Using the Bat

Cave's Bat Radar he was able to scan the exterior to the cave's entrance.

When he had determined the area was clear he jumped into the Batmobile and sped to the crime scene.

Deciding en route to reconnoiter rather than rush right in, Batman parked the Batmobile is a secluded area behind the bank, turning on and testing the ICD. When he stepped out of the car he saw that it worked perfectly. He left to check out the bank—how to get in, where the hostages were being held, and most importantly, how to defeat and capture the gunmen. During his absence Bat Girl swiftly approached the bank, unknowingly parking her Batgirl Cycle only a few feet from the invisible Batmobile. Like Batman, she snuck toward the bank. Batman, realizing he would need a supply of Bat Gas from the Batmobile trunk, returned to the car to find the motorcycle only feet away. This gave him an idea. He had long been an admirer of Batgirl's tight firm ass and her pert breasts, but he had never been

able to determine her secret identity or where she lived. Now he saw his chance. Opening a pouch on his utility belt, Batman removed a Bat Homer and applied its super sticky surface to the underside of the cycle's rear fender. The homer would tell him where Batgirl lived and lead him to her secret identity. Then he'd blackmail her to fuck him silly. Once she saw and touched his mammoth cock, she would not be able to resist him. Maybe he'd even had a threesome with her and Stephanie.

Batman retrieved the Bat Gas and trotted to the bank's rear wall. Using the Batarang and climbing rope he was soon entering through a skylight on the roof. Swiftly, he made his way toward the vault, the logical place to keep the hostages. Sure enough, he saw four of the gunmen there standing over the seven hostages. Removing one of the special Bat Grenades filled with Bat Gas from his utility belt he pulled the pin and rolled it toward the thieves. It exploded, spraying Bat Gas all over the vault area, instantly putting the gunmen and hostages

harmlessly to sleep. Now Batman, using a Bat Gas Mask, began his search for any additional gunmen. He found one as he turned a corner but before the gunman could act he was laid low by something thrown by Batgirl.

"Well done, Batgirl," the Caped Crusader exclaimed. "Have you seen any others?"

"Only one, Batman, and he's safely tied up by the front entrance. I assume that was a Bat Grenade filled with Bat Gas I just heard."

"Yes, all I have to do is phone Chief O'Hara to pick up this mob and we'll be all done here. He knew that as soon as he turned his back, Batgirl would disappear. But this time it wouldn't do her any good.

CHAPTER 3

Batman used his remote to disable the ICD, climbed in and followed the active Bat Homer on the Bat Scanner. Once it stopped he knew who Batgirl was—Barbara Gordon. It had stopped just at her apartment. When he arrived he again activated the ICD and used the Batarang to scale to outside of Barbara Gordon's building, stopping at her balcony. Climbing over the railing, Batman peeked through the drapes behind the sliding door. Yes! He could see Barbara changing out of her Batgirl costume. He used his Bat Sliding Door Disabler and replaced it in the utility belt before stepping silently into the apartment.

He was only a few feet behind Barbara when he said, "Good evening Batgirl, or should I say Barbara."

Batgirl was startled but kept her cool. "That's not a real costume, I just rented it for a party."

"Yes, and I see you are keeping it in a secret room along with a lot of other rented Batgirl eQuipment. But don't worry, your secret is safe with me."

"OK, Batman, but how'd you find me?"

"That will be my secret, but there will be some more secrets we will share together." Just the suggestion of sex with this minx was stiffening his cock, something Barbara seemed to notice.

"Oh no, Batman. There's no way I'm fucking you, even if you do seem to have a pretty big cock."

"Really, Barbara? How'd you like to open the Gotham Times tomorrow and see your secret identity spread all over page one?"

"You wouldn't!"

"I wouldn't want to, but I will if you don't come across. I've wanted that ass of yours for ages."

Barbara could see no way out of this dilemma. Who knows, she thought, maybe he'll actually be pretty good at it. So she acquiesced, "OK, Batman, you win." She stepped out of her robe revealing the body that many had drooled over for years. Batman's cock sprung to its full length in reply to the sight of her 34DD breasts. He stepped out of his Bat Boots and costume, keeping his cowl in place. There was no way he was giving up his secret identity the same night he had learned Batgirl's. When he dropped his

boxers Batgirl/Barbara gasped. She had never seen such a monster cock. She was drawn to it like iron to a magnet, yet she feared it would rip her apart. Then, overcome by her lust she decided she just didn't give a shit. She had to have that magnificent erection in her.

Barbara led him to the bedroom and sat him on the edge of her queen sized bed. Kneeling before him she took the colossus in her hand. Now, strangely, she wanted it even more. Despite its size she wrapped her lips around it. She used her tongue to lick all around the massive head; Batman groaned in response. Slowly Batgirl started moving up and down taking as much into her mouth as possible. If anything, the Batprick grew even longer and harder. Batman moved back onto the bed and motioned Batgirl to follow. It wasn't necessary; the sex crazed Batgirl wanted that cock and she was going to get it! Straddling Batman she slowly lowered herself onto the steel organ. It was even bigger than her biggest dildo, and she thought that was pretty fucking big. As

she lowered she felt her pussy walls stretching to accommodate the huge Batprick. The feeling was incredible as every nerve ending sang with excitement. Eventually she managed to get eight inches into her. Still she was not satisfied. She rose up and dropped suddenly, driving the steely post deep into her womb. Now she was able to rock and grind her clit hard against Batman. Batgirl knew she had long nipples; her clit was even longer. It was almost as long as Bruce's original erection so it didn't take much to stimulate it. Her lust boiled over as she came hard spraying Batman with her ejaculate. Batman took this as a signal to change positions and holes. He pushed Batgirl off and positioned her on her hands and knees at the edge of the bed. Again he slid his massive tool into her pussy, but once it was again well lubricated he removed it and repositioned at her ass.

Normally, Batgirl would have refused. She had never had anal and she didn't intend to, but she couldn't counter the magical effect of the Batprick. Instead of

denying him she pushed her ass back and opened her butt cheeks inviting the huge phallus to enter. Slowly Batman pushed himself into her ass. Batgirl screamed from the pain but she seemed powerless to deny him. In fact, the more it hurt, the more she wanted it. Eventually, he had forced himself past her sphincter and the pain subsided somewhat even though the prick slid deeper and deeper into her bowel. When his balls struck her ass he started to piston her ass hard. Batgirl's expressions of pain turned to grunts of pleasure, picking up speed as batman speeded his thrusts. Harder and harder they propelled each other toward climax. Batgirl sensed he was about to cum so she reached back to cradle his balls and said, "Oh yes, fuck me harder with that huge tool of yours. Fuck me and cum in my virgin ass. At this point Batman needed no more encouragement. He held her hips tightly and forced himself even deeper into her as he sprayed column after column of hot sperm up her ass. As he subsided she felt her second orgasm overtake and claim her. It shook her like a rag doll, forcing her to fall into a heap on the bed. When Batman pulled out she had a huge gape in her

asshole that would take over an hour to shrink back to normal. Barbara surprised even herself when she rose and licked the magnificent cock clean.

Batman looked at her, but before he could say anything she interrupted.

"I know what you're going to say so let me say it for you. Yes, we can do it again and, hopefully often. I don't understand it, but I just can't get enough of that wonderful colossal cock of yours. I'll ache tomorrow but it'll be well worth it."

Batman smiled, knowing that she was his to fuck forever. She'd never outgrow her need for his cock—never.

CHAPTER 4

Batman let his cock ooze semen all over barbara gordon's bed at least that was his intention. Barbara had already cleaned her pussy and ass juices from the magnificent Batprick, but there was still some sperm laden man juice leaking forth. When she saw it, Barbara ☐uickly rushed her tongue forward so she could lick and swallow every last drop. Eventually, Batman rose to dress and leave, but Barbara refused to release his cock. Batman walked toward the living room with Barbara Gordon shuffling along caressing and sucking him. While Batman dressed she continued to lick and kiss the huge beast. Batman recognized this behavior as the curse at its worst.

Before leaving the monastery years ago in Tibet the Lama had spoken to him, "You will find that all women, once they have seen or touched your member will want to mate with you, while others will refuse to allow you peace. They will haunt you in pursuit of your penis. That is the nature of the curse. That is also why we have so many monks here in this remote monastery." Bruce had found this to be true while in college. He was able to fuck every girl he dated once they discovered the size of his erection—Quite a change from his younger years—but some became obsessed with his manhood. Fortunately, at the end of the year they returned home some distance from Gotham City (that's why he never picked local girls). Since then he had been careful who he became involved with and his taking of Stephanie as a slave had served well to provide him with release. Stephanie's innate submissiveness meant that she would not be so assertive as to chase Bruce. Also, she knew she would be able to service him at least once every day.

Finally, Bruce managed to dress and push the wanton slut aside. "Please, Batman," she pleaded. "Can't we fuck again? Can't I suck you, lick you? Please put your gorgeous dick in my ass again. I have never cum like that before. It's like your cock is magic."

"You know I have to leave, Barbara. What would we do if your father Commissioner Gordon or Chief O'Hara needed me?"

"I could go in the Batmobile with you. I could suck your cock on the way there and on the way back," she pleaded again.

"I'll return when I can," he said cruelly. "Meanwhile, I'll think of some depraved sex acts we can do together. Maybe I'll piss on you. You'd like that, wouldn't you?"

"I'll take anything that comes from your wonderful cock—anything. Pee on me, jerk off on me-- anything!"

Batman left her crumpled in a heap on the floor. He slipped out to the patio and down the Batrope to the Batmobile. On the way back to the Batcave he was reminded that he still had to finish Stephanie's punishment—and then his favorite part—the after-punishment fun.

Batman used the reverse Batpole to propel himself back up to stately Wayne Manor. He stepped out into the study to find Stephanie there naked on her knees.

"I knew you would want to punish me further, Master. I want to show you how sorry I am, too."

"Very well," Bruce replied. "Come here, bend over the chair, and we'll finish this business."

Stephanie complied immediately, so eager was she to feel the ire of her Master. Bruce could see the handprints—red welts on her butt cheeks-- from the earlier spanking. He massaged and caressed her ass. It was the finest ass he had ever seen and the only one he had been driven to lick and eat. He grabbed the switch—a four foot sprig of willow—and applied it twice to her buttocks. When Stephanie started to cry he took her into his arms and soothed her. While they caressed she asked, "May I service you, Master?"

Bruce merely nodded so she dropped to her knees and began to remove his fine-tailored slacks. His erection was so strong from the combination of the punishment and the closeness of her lush body that it didn't just make a tent in his shorts, it pushed the leg of his boxers up past his crotch so it could stand free and erect. Stephanie licked his shaft starting at his balls, moving all the way up to the tip. Even though Barbara Gordon had licked him clean only an hour earlier, she was able to taste the other woman and

his cum. She would never complain—she was Bruce's slave, not his wife. Over the time they had been involved Stephanie had worked hard to deep throat Bruce's enormous phallus. She had thus far been able to get half of it into her mouth. Daily she did exercises to stretch her jaw muscles so she could accommodate him. Now she started to ingest his cock, actually getting seven inches into her mouth and throat. She licked and sucked him in and out of her wet hot mouth, tonguing him at every opportunity. She especially loved sticking her tongue into his pee hole and licking up any pee or cum that lingered. Bruce was amazed and amazingly turned on watching her perform oral on him. He started to groan, showing his pleasure at her actions. She quickened her pace, hoping he would cum in her mouth so she could taste and swallow his delicious semen. Bruce, however, had other ideas. He shrugged out of his shirt, pulled her up and kissed her deeply, tasting not only her sweet mouth but everything that had been on his manhood, as well. Then he bent her over the leather arm chair and retrieved some lube from a cabinet where he stored

all his sex supplies. He lubed his erection then put some onto and into her ass. She shivered in delight as he began to push his cock into her butt. Stephanie had been on the receiving end many times so her anus was well accustomed to his size. She leaned back spreading her cheeks to welcome him to her brown hole. Slowly, certainly, his cock squeezed into her. "Oh, thank you, Master. Thank you so much," she whispered. As Bruce started to thrust his cock she moved her ass back to maximize the depth of his penetration. Now he was balls deep—almost twelve inches into her bowel. Her tight sphincter pressed relentlessly against his erect cock and her bowel walls also stretched to handle him, making the entire experience incredibly intense. They continued their movements for several minutes, neither wanting it to end, but eventually biology and their mutual needs won out. Stephanie started to buck as her orgasm neared; Bruce's prick swelled even more signaling he was about to cum. "Turn around. I want to cum in your mouth," he commanded, fulfilling her dream. Quickly she pulled away and knelt again before him. She inhaled his cock savoring the taste of her own

ass as she started to milk him. She was still quivering in the initial throes of an orgasm and when he started to spurt thick ropes of cum into her throat she couldn't hold back. Her climax caused every part of her body to convulse, her mouth drawing even more semen from her Master, her lover. Eventually he collapsed into the chair and pulled her to him. She sat across his lap caressing his head and kissing him deeply as they recovered.

CHAPTER 5

Once he had recovered and dismissed Stephanie he started to think about Batgirl/Barbara. His darker side demanded that he humiliate her sexually. The only question was—how. Suddenly, the seed of an idea came to his fertile mind—an idea that would also get her and Stephanie together for a threesome. Unless

he was needed as Batman he would execute his plan tomorrow. Oh, joy.

The following morning he had his faithful butler Alfred summon Stephanie to the study at stately Wayne Manor. Of course, she came immediately. He outlined his plan to her. Initially she was hesitant to participate, but one stern look from Bruce returned her to her submissive ways. "Above all, you must not reveal that Batman is Bruce Wayne. Simply do as I instruct, regardless of what instructions I give. Do you understand?"

"Yes, Master. I will follow your instructions to the letter. I do not like sharing you, though. Will I get to fuck or suck you?"

"Yes, I think you will, but I will also expect you to interact with Barbara Gordon. Now here is my first instruction. At five o'clock you are to take some papers to her apartment. I work with her on the

Gotham City Orphanage Board so she won't suspect anything unusual, and I really do need her signature on some documents. It will take you almost a half hour to reach her apartment. While you are there I will sneak in from her patio. You will act surprised, but you will do as I instruct. Also, before you leave stately Wayne Manor you are not to empty your bladder. Got it?"

"Yes, Master. I will leave here at five o'clock sharp and I will not empty my bladder."

"One other thing, Stephanie—I will not need you this afternoon. You'll get plenty of attention at Barbara Gordon's."

Stephanie was disappointed but worked hard not to show it. "Yes, Master, as you command." She rose and left the room.

Bruce relaxed in the thick chair but he was so excited he couldn't help himself. He removed his cock from his pants and stroked it until hard. He thought about recalling Stephanie but decided against it. This way he'd be more than ready for the afternoon's games.

Time dragged for Bruce. He had his normal responsibilities dealing with the administration of his financial empire, of course, and he had to deal with problems that arose around stately Wayne Manor. Nonetheless, it seemed to take forever for five o'clock to arrive. Just after four he phoned Barbara Gordon to let her know that his secretary would be coming over shortly. Once that was done he opened the secret panel and descended to the Batcave. His ward Dick Grayson was home from school, so he wanted to come, but Batman dissuaded him. "Just taking the Batmobile for a little spin after tuning her up this morning," he lied. This was one time he definitely didn't want the Boy Wonder around.

Batman watched Stephanie leave through a security camera. True to her word it was five o'clock sharp. Then Batman climbed into the Batmobile and sped through the city. He saw Stephanie's car as he parked the Batmobile, activated the ICD, and scaled the wall to Barbara Gordon's apartment. He wasn't at all surprised to find the sliding door unlocked. He stepped through just has Barbara Gordon started to sign the first sheet.

"Well, I see I'll have two whores today."

Startled, Barbara Gordon turned toward Batman. Already, at his first words, her panties were becoming spotted with her feminine essence. "B...B...Batman?"

"Yes, who else would enter from the patio? I see you need some instruction in good manners. Who's your hot friend?"

"I'm Stephanie, secretary for billionaire Bruce Wayne, sir," Stephanie replied nervously. She was also getting wet. She loved when her Master was so dominant.

"Well, as long as you're here you'd better join us. Remove your clothing—both of you. I want some fun, and perhaps two will be better than one. Barbara, you go first. Let's see how fast you can become naked. If you want some of this cock, it had better be fast, real fast!"

Barbara wasted no time ripping her blouse, bra, and skirt from her body. Buttons were flying everywhere. When she was down to her now soaking panties she just tore them to shreds.

"Very well done, slut whore, now remove your friend's garments."

Both women looked uncomfortable, but for different reasons. Barbara Gordon had never been this close to another woman; Stephanie really had to pee. Barbara really wanted some of Batman's wonderful cock so she complied and started to disrobe Stephanie, starting at the top and moving down. When she was kneeling in front of Stephanie Batman said, "Go ahead, slut, I can see you really want some of that hot pussy. Just take a lick at it." Barbara Gordon looked at Batman who had stripped down to his cowl and cape. One look at his magnificent tool filled her with desire. She wanted some of that so she did as Batman commanded. She leaned in to Stephanie's mound and started to suck her juices.

"Uh, Batman, I really have to pee and all this licking is just making it worse." It was Stephanie, playing her role even better than Batman/Bruce could have hoped.

"Well, then, go ahead. Pee on Barbara. You want her to pee on you, don't you?"

"One more look at the Batprick and she would do anything...ANYTHING...to get some of it. "Y...Yes, I want your pee. Pee on my head and face."

Then she returned to licking Stephanie's swollen clit. That was all it took for Stephanie to release her pungent hot pee all over Barbara Gordon's face. The yellow stream ran down her neck and around her breasts before settling into the carpet. Barbara Gordon would remember this for a long time. Batman retrieved a towel from the kitchen just as Stephanie was reaching what he was sure would be her first of several powerful orgasms. Batgirl/Barbara had been playing with her own clit while she was eating Stephanie so she too was shaking with delight.

Batman threw the towel at Barbara Gordon. "Dry yourself, and you, Stephanie, isn't it? You lick her

pussy while she's cleaning up. I think you'll find it to your liking—almost as big as a cock. Suck it, and if you do a good job you can suck me later. Stephanie was still hot and she just loved her Master at his most dominant. She lowered herself to Barbara's cunt. Her clit was sticking out, almost horizontally, looking like a small cock. She definitely knew what to do with a cock, didn't she? She sucked it like she would a hard cock, sliding it into and out of her mouth. Batman reached up behind Barbara and probed her ass with two fingers. Barbara was in heaven. Suddenly Batman withdrew his fingers and led them to the bedroom. Once there he positioned Stephanie at the headboard telling Barbara to lick and eat her ass. Barbara attacked that sweet rear with gusto. She had never eaten an ass before and now, under the magical influence of the Batprick, she was wondering what had taken her so long. She knew what to do, of course. Batgirl could read! Now she put her knowledge to use. She began to lick all around Stephanie's rosebud. Once she was at ease, she pushed her tongue deep into Stephanie's anus. She loved the taste and aroma of this gorgeous butt. As

her tongue darted in and out of Stephanie, Batman moved behind her and positioned his enormous cock right at the entrance to her dark tunnel. He used no lube, wanting to cause the woman as much pain as pleasure. Barbara Gordon, once a widely known prude was now a total slut for Batman. She turned briefly, "Please Batman, fuck me hard in my ass. Make me scream with desire. Oh, God, please, please!"

Batman placed both hands on her hips and pushed – hard, ramming his rod of steel into her bowel. Barbara did scream as the pain built rapidly. But there was something special—magical—about this pain. It evolved to pure pleasure which spread from her butt through her entire body. It drove her to eat more actively of Stephanie's butt. She rammed her tongue into Stephanie's ass and moved her hand to her cunt, fingering her fast and hard. It wasn't long before all three felt orgasm approaching. Batman pistoned Barbara's ass harder and faster as his cock swelled even larger. Boiling up from his balls he shot

stream after stream of hot cum into Barbara Gordon's sweet ass. The sensation of his cum filling her already stuffed ass drove Barbara over the top. She shook once—hard—and felt the euphoria flood her body. Last, but not least, Stephanie could not resist Barbara's onslaught to her ass and pussy. She screamed as her orgasm struck her like a bolt of lightning, falling forward and pulling the others with her.

CHAPTER 6

It was almost an hour later that Batman first stirred, so powerful was his climax. He withdrew his still hard phallus from Batgirl/Barbara, leaving a gaping hole almost two inches wide. Barbara wanted more and more of the Batprick so she immediately followed Batman, groping for his manhood as he walked down

the hallway. At the living room she darted in front of him and took him into her mouth. She licked up one side and down the other, loving the taste of his cum mixed with the flavor of her own ass. As she knelt before him his semen ran out of her ass and down the inside of both thighs. "Wipe it with your finger and eat it," Batman commanded. Eagerly, she scooped her hand up each thigh and into her mouth. She loved the taste and texture of his man juice. When she had scooped it all up Batman spoke again. "Stick you fingers into your ass and empty it of my cum. Pour it into your mouth and lick your fingers clean. Again she complied and again she couldn't get enough. Eventually she returned her attentions to the Batprick. When it was clean he turned around and spoke again, "Clean my ass as you did to Stephanie."

Again, Barbara now turned into a complete slut to whom nothing was out-of-bounds, complied eagerly. In

her sexually intoxicated state she would willingly, no eagerly, do anything he asked. She licked all around

the Batman's sphincter before forcing her tongue into his ass as far as it could go. She tasted the sweet unmistakable flavor of him, loving every minute of it. Suddenly Batman spun around and forced his mammoth erection into her mouth and throat. She gagged but took as much of him as humanly possible. He mouth fucked her fast and hard to another fantastic orgasm just as Stephanie appeared in the room. "Come here," he said to her. "Take any sperm that leaks from her mouth into your own." Swiftly Stephanie joined Barbara on the floor just as Batman spurted several huge ropes of semen into her mouth. No woman alive could have swallowed that much cum so it leaked out the corners of her mouth where Stephanie slurped it up joyfully. When he was done Batman turned, dressed, and disappeared out the patio door.

Stephanie was still licking Barbara's face, cleaning it of any remaining cum. Looking into Barbara's eyes she leaned back and asked, "Does this happen often?"

"Not often enough," replied Barbara, "Not often enough."

CHAPTER 7

Billionaire Bruce Wayne was leaning against the old leather chair in his study in stately Wayne Manor. It was just past 3 p.m. so, of course, his secretary/sex slave Stephanie knelt naked before him with the magnificent Batprick solidly in her mouth, her

sensational breasts pressing against his knees. She had an incredible body-34D-24-34 with an even more incredible mound just above her bare pussy. Bruce often wondered how she could get so much of his tool—almost 12 inches long and three inches wide—into her mouth. One of the other servants had told him that she had seen Stephanie exercising her jaws. Maybe that was it. Anyway you looked at it though she was a super cock sucker. Right now she had almost eight inches into her throat and was licking the enormous organ all over with each and every stroke. Bruce had only two things on his mind—should he fuck her pussy or ass before cumming in her mouth and what to do next with Batgirl. Since he had learned her secret identity he had striven to sexually humiliate her. First, he had blackmailed her to fuck him and taken her anal cherry, and second, he had her eat Stephanie's ass while he fucked her ass with his terrific tool. Whether he had caused her more pain or pleasure he wasn't sure. Now he needed another scenario. But first he needed to finish himself with his slave. Bruce pulled her to her feet and kissed her. She pushed her tongue into his

mouth where he could taste his own sex. He broke the kiss and she bent voluntarily over the chair arm. "Please, Master, she purred. "Please fuck my ass. I love it when you fuck my ass."

Bruce was in a really good mood because of his recent conquests of Batgirl. He wanted to satisfy her as much as he wanted to be satisfied. He positioned his monster cock at her ass. First he inserted two fingers, rubbing them in and out. "Oh, thank you, Master. Thank you so much." He had fucked Stephanie's ass so many times she was always ready for it. He pushed his head against her anus until it yielded, using her slippery cunt juice as lubricant. He went in with an audible "POP" then slid in until his balls rested against her slit and clit. Now he humped and his every thrust was met by her hips moving in the opposite direction. The combined action of her sphincter and bowels soon began to milk him. Stephanie could feel his cock quiver and pulse. "May I swallow your cum, Master?" He withdrew and immediately rammed his cock deep into her throat

just in time to spray rivers of hot cum deep into her belly. She moved his erection slightly out so she could lick the tip and taste the cum as it flowed into her mouth. Once she was sure the flow of cum had ended she washed all traces of her ass from his shrinking erection. When Bruce had withdrawn she asked, "May I service you again please, Master?" It was tempting but he wanted to save himself for tonight's session with the Batbitch. Instead he asked, "Did you enjoy our session with Barbara Gordon?"

"Oh yes, Master. I loved it when she ate my ass, but not as much as when you did it."

"Well, perhaps we'll set something up again. You did well not to reveal that I am Batman, very well indeed."

Batman/Bruce was determined to totally destroy Barbara Gordon. Bruce had asked her out several times while they were in high school together and she

had blown him off every time, ridiculing his dinky dick as only a high school girl could do. That's when he had first plotted his revenge. He knew what he wanted to do now but wasn't quite sure how to arrange it. When in doubt he thought, use the direct approach. It had been more than two weeks since the threesome with Stephanie. Batman had seen Batgirl once in that time at a crime scene and she was obviously hungry for some more of the Batprick. She would have blown him right there in front of the cops if he would have let her. Well, she could have some of it tonight, he thought, and some more cock, too. Ha ha!

CHAPTER 8

It was almost midnight when Batman scaled the wall to Barbara Gordon's apartment balcony. Once again the sliding door was unlocked. She really was getting desperate. Batman let himself in and removed his costume. He stood there in his cowl and cape, muscled body and huge cock reflecting the dim light from the street. He went to the front door, opened it, placed the whistle to his lips, and blew. Soon his companion joined him in the apartment. Now they snuck to Barbara's bedroom.

Barbara was sound asleep until the light was suddenly on. "Who's there? What's going on?" she shouted sleepily.

"No need to yell, Barbara," Batman replied calmly. "I was a little horny this evening and I knew you would want to suck me off, so here I am."

Barbara rubbed her eyes seeing Batman and his companion, a large brown dog that looked like a

Great Dane who was wearing leather booties on its paws. She looked at Batman, "What's with the...," but then she suddenly got it. "Oh no, I'm not doing any dog."

"Just come here and rub my cock, Barbara. Then we'll talk about it," said Batman Quietly, knowing that as soon as she made contact with his erection, the curse would take over stronger than ever. Barbara was amazed every time she saw it. It has so huge she couldn't believe it could ever support itself. She reached out and gently stroked the underside of the lengthy shaft. As she did her yearning grew into desire. When she placed both small hands around it that desire grew into lust—wanton lust. Batman sat on the edge of bed and positioned Barbara so she was standing just in front of him, bent at the waist, legs apart. The dog's interest grew in proportion to her wetness, becoming motivated by the female scent of her secretions. Was this a bitch to be bred? He reached his tongue between her legs to taste her, the roughness of its tongue stimulating her slit and

clitoris. The more he licked, the wetter she got; the wetter she got, the more he licked.

"Ooh, that feels incredible," Barbara moaned, her words almost unintelligible as she sucked away on the Batman's huge tool.

Batman spoke. He wanted to direct the activity. "Suck harder on my cock, Barbara. Take me deeply into your mouth."

When, she started to blow him in earnest, Batman continued. "Stroke the dog. Bring his penis out from its sheath." Because of the curse Barbara was unable to resist. She closed her legs and moved so her hand could reach the dog's balls. She caressed and rubbed them. As the dog became more and more excited his erection grew dramatically from its sheath to a full thick fourteen inches. "Go ahead, touch it. Stroke it."

Barbara reached down, feeling the dog's hardness. His cock was covered in slippery precum. She was tentative at first, but her lust was driving her actions. She would do anything to enjoy Batman's cock. With her left hand she was stroking Batman while she licked and sucked up and down his shaft. Her right hand began stroking the dog faster and harder. Now was the time, Batman decided. He repositioned her onto the bed so her hips and legs hung over one side of the bed and her head hung over another at a right angle. He moved the eager dog so his forefeet were on the bed and the tip of its cock was just outside Barbara's pussy. He fingered Barbara hard and fast, increasing her wetness, and rubbed his finger across the dog's wet nose. The dog lunged forward driving almost four inches, roughly thirty percent, of its cock into Barbara's cunt. Frantically, the dog drove its cock into her, its pointed tip pushing into her womb. All the dog knew was that it wanted to impregnate this bitch. He rammed his cock forward until his knot was wedged into her. Barbara screamed both in pain and in pleasure as the knot swelled and sealed her canal. Batman now attacked the other orifice with his

monster. He pushed about two inches into her waiting mouth then forced even more into her, fucking her mouth hard and fast. She gagged several times but continued licking and sucking. There was no way she was giving up her prize. She loved this cock and would do anything to have it, as evidenced by her coupling with the canine.

Batman felt his balls boil so he pushed even deeper into Barbara's eager mouth. When she sucked him strongly he couldn't resist. Long spurts of hot cum flooded her mouth and throat. "Swallow all of it slut," Batman instructed. That was one directive that was unnecessary; Barbara had no intention of letting any get away. Meanwhile the dog was making rapid short strokes intent on flooding her with his semen. He stopped suddenly as jets of his cum drowned her womb and tunnel. "Oh my God!!!" Barbara exclaimed when she could finally speak, "I've never felt so filled up. It's incredible, unbelievable. Who would have thought a dog…"

Barbara licked Batman's phallus clean while waiting for the knot to subside. Doggy cum started to pour from her cunt. Batman grabbed her hand and directed it to some of the leakage. Using her hand he scooped some onto her fingers and moved it to her mouth. "Lick," he said. Slowly she extended her tongue. Finding that she loved the taste, she eagerly scooped up every drop, even dipping into her swollen cunt. Batman looked at her. "You're not done yet, clean his cock. You don't think I want a dog with a dirty cock in the Batmobile, do you? If you do, I'll give you the fucking you want so badly. You do want it, don't you?"

"You know I do, you bastard. I hate you; I love you. I can't do without you. I used to be such a prude. When I think of all the time I wasted...." Barbara went down to the floor. By lying on her side she was able to lick the doggy dong. Only one problem, the more she licked the harder it grew. The beast was ready to fuck her again.

Batman lay back on the bed slowly stroking his gargantuan cock, keeping it ready for what was to come next. When Barbara was finished with the dog he pulled her on top of him. Her cunt was running with the combined fluids of the dog and herself. He rammed his mammoth dong deep into her. He wasn't as long as the dog but he was much wider. Barbara groaned audibly in the initial pain, but her expression rapidly turned to one of pleasure. Batman snapped his fingers getting the dog's attention. He signaled the beast onto the bed behind Barbara, its huge cock swung freely. Batman grabbed it pushing it up against her ass. "Oh no, please. Don't let him fuck my ass. It's too big. It's too fucking big," Barbara begged. Ignoring her, Batman snapped his fingers again. The dog lunged forward forcing his slippery hard-on right into her ass. "Unghh, I'm being split in two. Please stop, please!" Barbara was pleading. Again, Batman snapped his fingers and again the dog lunged. Now its knot was banging up against Barbara's anus. This was going to be a battle between the tightness of her asshole and the determination of the dog to mate. Assholes are

strong, but apparently not as strong as a big dog. The beast pushed with all its strength forcing the knot past the sphincter. Barbara screamed continuously until Batman clamped his hand over her mouth. Even then she screamed until the dog began to move. The rapidity of its thrusts, much faster than any human cock, started to drive her crazy. She'd never experienced anything like it. The friction on her bowel walls combined with the action of the famous Batprick brought her swiftly to a powerful orgasm that never seemed to end. Over and over the grip of the orgasm ran through her body until the dog ceased its movements and jetted buckets of hot doggie cum up her bowel. The action of the dog combined with Barbara's orgasm brought Batman again to a searing climax. He poured rope after thick rope of hot cum into her pussy. Eventually, she collapsed onto him as the knot popped from her butt and the dog withdrew.

She lay there for some time with Batman caressing her. She roused herself, took his flaccid penis in her

hand and began kissing it. She licked his balls and moved up to the head, cleaning him as she went. She took his entire cock into her mouth and stimulated him back to hardness. Now SHE was in control. She probed his ass with first one and then two fingers. When she removed them she licked them clean. "I like that almost as much as I like the taste of your cock...and I love that. When you first came here I hated you for everything you made me do. But now I see that you've opened my eyes to a whole new world of sensational sexual experiences. I've had more orgasms—much bigger orgasms-- in the past three weeks than I had in the previous five years." Batman realized then that his plans to embarrass and humiliate her had failed. On the positive side, he did have a new slave—a new source of sexual gratification.

Batgirl/Barbara continued to stroke him. A new sense of arousal overcame him. He wanted to cum again, and badly. He needed to dominate her again. "Sit on

it. Push it into your ass and then fuck me with it. Fuck me hard."

Barbara squatted above him and lowered herself onto his huge erection, wondering once again how it could possibly fit. But she was controlled by the curse. There was nothing she could do. She had to have that cock and if it split her ass, so be it. It was a struggle getting past her sphincter so in her lust Barbara rose up and dropped herself suddenly forcing the cock up into the bowel. There was pain and lots of it, but also there was pleasure. As she continued the pain ebbed and the pleasure rose. She found herself in a state of sexual euphoria. She rocked back and forth, back and forth, rubbing the cock against her sphincter and bowel walls. The feeling was better than the best shit she'd ever taken, in fact she knew that she had never felt better in her entire life. She felt Batman's thick cock swell and quiver as he came for the second time and sprayed her with his man juice. She clenched her ass muscles as she started to cum again and again and again. Her body was

drenched in sweat from her exertions. She fell into a heap totally exhausted. As Batman rose to leave she tried to speak. "Next time... bring... two... dogs...please," just before she passed out.

CHAPTER 9

Batman decided to walk out of Barbara's apartment at 3 a.m. rather than climb down the rope. He had to let the dog out that way anyway. He strolled leisurely from the building, entered the Batmobile, and drove away. He started to think about what had gone wrong. Batgirl/Barbara should have been embarrassed, humiliated, destroyed by all she had been forced to do. But she wasn't. All Batman had done was release her inner slut, and she definitely was a super slut. Was there anything she wouldn't do? Maybe he should have the dogs pee on her. Would that do it? Probably not, he concluded. She'd probably drink it. Batman was in a real Quandary when he drove unseen into the Batcave.

Rising up the reverse Batpole he exited in the study. He was surprised to fine his slave Stephanie waiting for him. As usual, she was kneeling and she was naked. "Oh, Master, I'm so glad you are home. I know you were with that Barbara again. I know I can service you better than she can. Just give me a chance to prove it to you...please."

Batman/Bruce gave that some thought, then came to a decision. "Come with me, Slave, let's go to bed." He rarely took her to bed, preferring to have her every afternoon, but tonight he was wired after the evening's events and what better to help him relax that some Master/Slave sex? He lifted her to her feet and put his arm around her. "You haven't had any orgasms since our last time together, have you? I wouldn't want to have to punish you."

"Oh no, Master. I have wanted to cum badly—really badly—but I have waited for you. I love to cum with you, Master."

Bruce smiled. It was going to be a good night, after all. He had enjoyed the sex with the Batslut but he had been pissed that he had failed to destroy her. He would use Stephanie's lush body to turn everything right.

When they arrived at Bruce's bedroom suite he dropped his soiled clothes on the floor and led his slave to the shower. She grabbed the soap and started to wash his body, planning to start at his shoulders and work her way down to his humongous rod which she planned to clean with her tongue. Unfortunately, she was the slave so she was overruled immediately. Bruce pulled her into a deep passionate kiss as the hot steamy water rolled over their bodies. Bruce took the soap and sudsed her body concentrating on her magnificent ass—the ass that had gotten her through college. He rubbed and massaged her butt cheeks taking time to insert some soap into her ass. She shrieked with pleasure at his touch. He just gave her a look and she knew what he

wanted. She turned and bent to grab her ankles, placing that delectable ass at just the right height and angle for his mammoth member. He soaped it and pushed it against her ass. Surprise!! Suddenly, she backed up against him, impaling her butt on his cock. She backed again pushing him against the shower wall where she started to ass fuck herself at a frantic pace. Bruce had never seen her so aggressive; he liked it. In fact, he loved it. She fucked him fast and hard using the shower door for leverage. Even after cumming three times with the Batslut and once with Stephanie earlier in the day, he felt a rumbling in his groin. It was slow rising, but it came on steadily until he couldn't control it. His cock started to ☐uiver in anticipation. Stephanie knew that feeling as well as he did. She pulled off, reversed, and knelt intending to take it in her mouth. She was just a little slow. His first jet hit her in the hair and face; the second right on her nose. But she got the third right on her tongue. By the time the fourth came she had safely enclosed his cock in her hot mouth. She swallowed all she could and washed the rest away. She closed the shower, dried Bruce's exhausted body and led him to

bed. She climbed in next to him, embracing his body until they fell asleep.

CHAPTER 10

Bruce Wayne awoke in the late morning to find Stephanie, his secretary/sex slave naked in bed with him, her knee in his crotch, her head on his chest. He had a vague recollection of a shower and feeling euphoric, but nothing else. When he looked at Stephanie he saw her eyes were open. She smiled, moved her free hand to his flaccid cock and stroked it to hardness. Her hands slid over the length of his cock; soon he was fully erect. She looked at her Master," May I, Master?" she whispered, kissing his nipple. He nodded and she lowered her head onto his shaft. She licked up and down, as well as all around his tip and pee hole, rapidly bringing him to a state of high arousal. He shifted Stephanie around and over

his body so he could taste her. He moved his tongue from her butt hole, up her moist slit, and ending on her clit. She was delicious. Her juices flowed from within her, only to be lapped up by the superhero. She started to buck as her excitement rose and her cock sucking efforts grew more frantic. Bruce moistened two fingers and plunged them into her ass, using them to fuck her anus hard. Next he sucked and nibbled on her clit. She started to ▢uiver. Suddenly, her body shook as a powerful orgasm claimed her. She tingled from head to toe and fell exhausted to the bed.

"That wasn't fair, Master," she gasped. I'm supposed to service you."

"You can have your chance as soon as you recover," he said as a smile broke out on his face. She's had a sensational orgasm, but now she'd pay for it. "Moisten a finger and push it into my ass. Move it around, in and out. I want it to feel good. Oh, that's

wonderful; now another finger." A few seconds later, "Good, very, very good. Now take them out and clean them in your mouth." Obediently, Stephanie removed her fingers. They had a pungent sweet smell as she plunged them unhesitatingly into her mouth. Licking them with her tongue cleaned them in an instant. She held them for Bruce's inspection. He was satisfied with her work so far. "Again, but this time push your fingers deeper into my ass. I'll tell you when to take them out." Again she followed his orders explicitly. After five minutes in his ass he told her to once again suck and lick them. Stephanie didn't particularly like doing this but she had agreed to follow her Master's orders no matter how repulsive or disgusting. She was determined to be the best slave ever. While she had her fingers in her mouth Bruce asked her, "Stephanie you're a bright girl. Why did you sleep your way through Gotham Tech instead of just doing the work?"

Stephanie kept working her fingers until they were spotless and odorless. She just looked at Bruce and

calmly explained. "It's easy, I'm a slut. I love to fuck. I love to suck. I love anal. And most of all I love being submissive to a dominant male, although I suppose a dominant female would be OK, too. May I ask, Master, how you knew all about that?"

"Yes, you can ask. But first, let's have another round. Stick those fingers in me." When she had complied he continued, "I graduated from Gotham Tech and I am their biggest benefactor. How much do I donate every year?"

She was still working her fingers in his ass as she answered, "Last year it was $25 million and the year before I think it was even more."

"You'd be surprised how much confidential information becomes public when you throw money in front of people. Your instructors just couldn't wait to tell all about their indiscretions with you when I offered to sponsor some research or buy some

ridiculously expensive piece of equipment. You can take them out now."

Bruce exited the bed just as she began to clean her fingers. She knew she could cheat and use the sheet, but she wouldn't. She had her pride as a slave. A knock on the door brought the upstairs maid, a 19-year old named Marianne into the room. She started when she saw Stephanie naked and was about to leave when she heard Bruce Wayne call from the bathroom. "Don't leave, Marianne. I think you should join us." She closed the door and crossed slowly to the bed. When Bruce appeared naked she turned red in embarrassment. "Stand up, let me take a close look at you." She rose and turned around before him. Most men would have described her as HOT. She was shorter than Stephanie—maybe 5 feet, 5 inches tall and just over 100 pounds. She had a small frame but nicely shaped buttocks, an ample bust, and an athletic-looking body. "Let's get you out of these clothes." Stephanie, finished now with her fingers, came to assist. The young girl didn't know how to

react. She stood there dumbfounded. Slowly her clothes were peeled from her body. Then Bruce led her to the bed. Marianne was no prude—she'd had boyfriends in high school and had plenty of sex, most of which wasn't very satisfying-- and she had heard stories about her employer, but she had never believed them until today. She had averted her eyes from his nakedness, but now that he was so close she couldn't avoid looking at the amazing thing that hung from where a penis should have been. No man, she thought, could possibly have a cock so big, so attractive, so intoxicating. Now that she had seen it she couldn't wait to touch it, bringing the curse to fruition.

Stephanie pulled the young girl to her and kissed her. It was Marianne's first woman-to-woman kiss and she loved it. She opened her mouth in response to the softness of Stephanie's lips and the probing of her tongue. Together they moved to either side of the magnificent member between Bruce Wayne's legs. Each took a side to lick and kiss; Marianne found that

she loved the taste and texture of him. She had never known a cock so hard. It was like mouthing a fleshy piece of steel. More than anything she wanted this cock in her pussy. She rose up and straddled Bruce, positioning herself over the beast before slowly lowering herself, gradually stretching herself around the huge cock. "Oh, my God. I can't believe this. It's so fucking big. I love it. Fuck me with it, Mr.Wayne. Please fuck me hard." Stephanie knew what she was feeling although she didn't know about the curse. Bruce, on the other hand, knew he could fuck this girl any time he wanted. This would be the first of many threesomes. He started to thrust, raising his hips and driving the cock deeper and deeper into the girl's cunt. Stephanie laid her head on Bruce's abdomen so she could lick Marianne's clit and she rode Bruce. Marianne's cunt was drenching Bruce and Stephanie was slurping it up as fast as it came. Suddenly the girl stopped moving. Her eyes glazed over. She started panting. Her orgasm was coming on strong and there was no stopping it. Just as suddenly she started bucking on the tool—faster and faster, harder

and harder—until she screamed in ecstasy and collapsed onto Bruce. Batman had conquered again.

Bruce thought she was done, but she was just a kid. She recovered ☐uickly, wanting more. Like Batgirl/Barbara Wayne she couldn't get enough of his mammoth manhood and she would do anything, absolutely anything to get it. When she roused herself Bruce positioned her on her hands and knees at the edge of the bed. He slid his cock into her pussy. "No one has a cock like this. Oh, you're going to ruin me for anyone else ." Funny-- that was exactly what he had in mind, having two slaves. He wondered how she would react to having it in her ass—hmmm! He slid two fingers into the tightly stretched cunt, lubing them for exploration of her ass. Once wetted, he pushed one and then two into her asshole. At first she started to protest but the pleasure of the Batprick in her cunt and the fingers up her ass made it impossible for her to complain. She was surprised when he withdrew and even more surprised when he began pushing it into her butt.

"No, Mr. Wayne. No. It'll never fit. You'll hurt me. I've never done anything like that. I'm a good girl."

"You mean you WERE a good girl. If you want some more of this cock you'll take it in your ass and love it. In fact, you'll beg me for it." Just then he managed to force the head past her sphincter. The girl screamed in agony. Undeterred, Bruce pushed further into her bowel. As he pushed the pain started to ebb and the pleasure rose. Soon she was humping back, driving her ass onto the rod. Bruce piled deeper and deeper into her until all his length was buried up her shitter. As he pumped her he reached around and grabbed her big swollen clit. He twisted and pulled it. The pain in her clit and the pleasure in her ass brought her higher and higher. Bruce was also almost ready to cum. His balls were boiling cum; his prick started to swell even more. The young girl was inexperienced, but not that inexperienced—she knew he was going to cum. The idea that he would do it in her ass drove her to an all-encompassing orgasm. Bruce drove long ribbons of cum up her ass. When he withdrew cum

ran out her gape down toward her pussy. Stephanie moved her head between the girl's legs and drank. Marianne didn't want to be cheated. She wiped with her fingers and slurped up every drop Stephanie missed, going so far as to finger her ass and lick the drippings. Marianne dressed and began to tidy the room when Bruce spoke, "Be at the study at three o'clock sharp and make sure you have removed your panties before you get there." Marianne would be getting a raise.

CHAPTER 11

Batman/Bruce still had to work something out for Barbara Gordon, aka Batslut. She had been a big surprise. For years she had been a "paragon of virtue," serving as a model of proper dignified behavior and restraint for the city's youth. She had preached abstinence and safe sex. How could he have known she was such a total fucking slut. He hadn't anticipated the power the curse held over her.

It seemed to work that way, now that he thought about it. Stephanie, who was admittedly a slut was less impacted by the curse, perhaps because it wasn't necessary with her. But a prude with an international reputation like Barbara Gordon succumbed to the power of the curse. He recognized the curse in Marianne's behavior; he wondered how strong it would be with her.

Eventually, he thought of something. Yes, he thought, that would definitely be fun. The only problem was where. Barbara's apartment was too small and he obviously couldn't use stately Wayne Manor. Of course—the farm. It would take about a day to coordinate everything. He phoned Barbara Gordon being sure to use the Bat Voice Disguiser.

"Hello, Barbara Gordon," she answered after the fourth ring.

"Have you recovered from the other night?"

"Who is this?" she demanded.

"Let's just say I know how much you love dogs."

"Batman?"

"Who else? I want to set something up with you—something we can't do in your apartment."

"Uh...will there be any...dogs there?"

"Yes, dogs, and maybe something else, too."

"Something else? "

"Yes, now I need you to do something for me. Call that other girl, what was her name? Tell her you need to meet her at your apartment at eight sharp tomorrow night. Then bring her with you to the old abandoned farm on Route 43. You know the one?"

"Yes, I know where it is, but what if she won't come with me?"

"She will. She wants some Batcock as much as you do. You do want it, don't you?"

"Damn you, Batman, you know I love that thing you have. I don't understand it either. I've never been so affected by the sight or touch of anything like that before."

"That's because there isn't anything else like it. It's one of a kind. Be at the farm by nine." He hung up the phone.

He summoned Stephanie and Marianne to the study. He already knew that Stephanie would do whatever he wanted so he needed to speak with Marianne.

"Marianne, did you enjoy yourself this morning?" he asked.

"Yes sir."

"Would you like to do stuff like that again?"

She was nervous. She didn't want to blow this. Actually, she definitely did want to blow and suck and fuck and take it in her ass. She wanted and needed more. "Y...yes s...sir."

"Good, Stephanie and I would love to include you in our little circle. But there would have to be some rules."

"OK, Sir."

"For one thing when it comes to sex you would be my slave, as is Stephanie. She has agreed to do anything I ask without hesitation." The young girl looked at Stephanie in amazement. "You will find that being my slave has many advantages. Right, Stephanie?

"Oh, yes, Master," she replied. "I love being your slave."

"Have you ever refused me any request?"

"Oh, no, Master! I would never do that. I love serving you."

"What were you doing when Marianne interrupted us this morning?"

"I stuck several fingers up your asshole and massaged your anus and prostate. Then I sucked and licked my fingers clean. I did it three times before she entered the bedroom."

"Could you do that Marianne? Would you do that?" If you do you can suck and fuck my cock almost every day. You would have threesomes with Stephanie and me regularly. Can you stay overnight?"

"Yes sir, I'm an orphan. I live alone in a dingy apartment. I can do it, sir. Will you give me a chance?"

"Very well, remove your clothing and come here."

Marianne stepped out of her maid outfit and removed her bra and panties, reminding Bruce to tell her that she would no longer wear panties while in stately Wayne Manor. "Stephanie, show her your panties." Stephanie lifted her skirt and showed her bald pussy and bare ass to the younger girl. "Stephanie, what happens if you wear panties in the house?"

"You punish me. I deserve to be punished for doing something so bad. You spank me."

"Are you allowed to give yourself orgasms without my permission?"

"No, Master. I don't need to. You give me more than enough orgasms ."

Marianne stood before Bruce Wayne naked. She knelt before him, "I will be thrilled to serve you, Mr. Wayne...I mean Master."

"Crawl over here and remove my pants and shorts. She crawled and carefully pulled down his clothing. "Moisten your fingers and stick two up my ass." Marianne was really nervous; she knew what was coming next. Could she do it? She put two fingers in her mouth, licking them; then carefully put them into her new Master's ass. She rubbed them all around. She didn't really know what to do but figured if she did enough some of it would be right. Now came the moment of truth. "Put your fingers in your mouth and clean them. She knew if she hesitated she would fail so she plunged the fingers into her mouth. She found it wasn't too bad. In a few seconds she thought they would be clean enough to pass inspection.

"You will follow Stephanie's lead. Not only is she older than you, her experience is worlds ahead of yours.

Now you will show her fealty by licking and eating her ass." Stephanie reclined over the arm of the old chair, revealing her beautiful ass. Bruce led the girl and showed her what to do. First, he licked her rosebud, then Marianne followed suit. Bruce pushed her away so he could push his tongue into Stephanie's anus. She squealed with pleasure. When he withdrew Marianne took his place. She learned how much pressure was needed to penetrate the anus and how to lick the interior walls. She found it remarkably tolerable. She kept it up for almost fifteen minutes until Stephanie had a very satisfying orgasm.

While they rested Bruce explained what would happen tomorrow night, how Barbara Gordon would call Stephanie to her apartment. Stephanie would take Marianne with her and both would accompany Barbara to the farm.

"Excuse me, Master," Stephanie interrupted, "Why the farm?"

"Because I cannot hope to deal with the three of you at once; we will need some other cocks—cocks that won't tell about it afterwards."

Marianne looked confused but Stephanie smiled. "Does that mean...?"

"Yes, I will bring some dogs, enough to deal with all of you."

Marianne looked horrified but Stephanie reassured her. "Fucking a dog is an experience to die for. Our Master has a magnificent cock but even he cannot fuck like a dog. You will have to trust me. I'll tell you all about it later—when we retire. You will stay in my room from now on so I can train you to serve and please our Master."

CHAPTER 12

Bruce was accustomed to sleeping alone, but for the second straight morning he had company in bed-- Stephanie on his left side and Marianne on his right.

He looked up to see his two slaves returning his gaze. "May we serve you, Master?" asked Marianne. Apparently, Stephanie had worked hard to train her in the few hours since their meeting the previous afternoon. When Bruce nodded they rolled him onto his side. Stephanie took his morning wood into her mouth; Marianne first kissed and licked his balls, then moved back to his sphincter. She licked his asshole like a person dying of thirst in the desert attacks an oasis waterhole.

She hungered for the taste of his ass. She pushed her probing tongue into and through the tight muscle so she could taste what lay beyond. She licked and sucked his bowel clean, and when she was done she licked her lips and went back for more. Bruce Wayne, aka Batman, was stimulated at both ends of his being. Stephanie had almost nine inches of his humongous sex organ down her throat, breathing only when she moved the monster on the outstroke. This continued for almost ten minutes. He grunted and started to pant, sure signs that his orgasm

neared. He pulled their heads closer to him as his first river of cum exploded into Stephanie's mouth. Realizing that his orgasm had arrived, Marianne moved quickly to get some of the yummy syrup for herself.

Bruce lay back while his slaves competed for his cum. He enjoyed watching them lick him clean then exchange his cum between their mouths. It pleased him to see their cooperation. "You may lick each other to orgasm," he said. "Thank you, Master. Thank you."

They were both hot to cum. They crawled all over each other getting into 69 with Marianne on top. Legs apart, heads forward into each other's cunts, the slurping began in earnest. It was a contest to see who could make the other cum first. Ultimately, Stephanie's age and experience won out. Marianne clamped her thighs tightly around Stephanie's head as she ground her cunt into her mentor's face. When

Stephanie nibbled on her clit she was overcome with ecstasy. She writhed in the throes of her climax, but was still able to get Stephanie off by sucking hard on her clit, forcing it between her teeth. They both collapsed on the bed, sweaty and drained in front of Bruce who thoroughly enjoyed the show. "Thank you, Master. I really needed that." It was Marianne, his new slave. "Yes, Master, me too," Stephanie added.

Bruce was busy all day making the arrangements for the evening's fun, stopping once when he was summoned by Commissioner Gordon to help stop a hostage situation in a fast food restaurant. Batgirl was also there. When they passed she reached out and cupped his manhood. Her glance told him she couldn't wait for tonight, either.

Barbara Gordon phoned Stephanie around 4 p.m. with the invitation that was promptly accepted. All was in readiness. Barbara was surprised when Stephanie showed up with another younger woman.

She could see that both were dressed in really hot, tight outfits, their long hair draped over their shoulders. When Barbara suggested they go for a ride she was surprised again at how eagerly they agreed. They went to the farm in Stephanie's car. At the farm they found the place deserted, or so it seemed. When they got to the house there was a small sign with an arrow to guide them. They arrived at an apparently deserted barn deep on the property. Batman opened the door to a lighted interior as they exited the car. As instructed, the two younger women—Batman's shills-- acted surprised to see him. Marianne played her role perfectly. "Batman? What's going on here?" she asked. Stephanie took her arm, leading her forward. "Don't worry. We're all going to have a really good time." Once in the barn Batman closed and locked the door. Even though it seemed rickety it was, in fact, a contemporary modular building, both light and sound proof. Inside were several benches covered with leather, restraints at each corner. Batman exposed himself, invoking the curse, as the women looked on in awe.

"Strip and take your place on one of the benches. Do it if you want some of this cock."

Mesmerized by the strength of the curse and the size of his magnificent phallus, each woman dropped her clothes on the straw-covered floor and moved to a bench. Stephanie went face down on the first; the others went on their backs. Marianne took the third bench leaving the center to Batgirl. Batman quickly shackled them to the benches. He walked from one to another as he disrobed, allowing them to lick him and rub his cock against their bodies. This reinforced the curse, rendering them defenseless to whatever he had in mind for them. When he opened a door, also soundproof, they could hear the dogs in their kennels. Fear came to Marianne's face but Stephanie and Barbara merely smiled. They knew what to expect and couldn't wait. Batman released three of the dogs—the Great Dane and two Dobermans. The Great Dane reserved Barbara as his own bitch. He had mated her before; she was his property. Each dog started to sniff and lick the cunt before him. The

licking quickly aroused the three women, but Marianne was most affected. It was driving her wild, bringing her to heights she had never yet known. Little did she realize there was much more to come. Batman watched the three women squirm in agony and ecstasy.

He walked to Barbara and dangled his cock in her face. Eagerly, she swallowed what she could and licked his tool feverishly. He could see the need in her eyes, yet the dogs did not mount. They continued to lick cunt and ass, driving the three women higher and higher.

Batman drew a whistle to his lips and blew. Obediently the dogs withdrew. The women begged for more. "Please let it fuck me. Please, I want it in my ass. Please, I need it. Please." When he felt they had suffered enough he blew again bringing the dogs back to the benches. Up went their front paws as they sprayed their bitches with precum. They lunged forward forcing their cocks up the pussies again and again until the knots were at the pussy doors. The

final thrust pushing the knots home were received with screams of pain as the pussies were stretched beyond even super-normal limits. Marianne cried out, "Make him stop. Make him stop!" The dogs were relentless, humping in overdrive. Stephanie and Barbara were euphoric and eventually even Marianne came to love the feeling in her cunt. Batman now released the other dogs, all nine of them, their pricks swinging in the air. Unable to mate they sought out whatever orifice they could find. They rammed their rods into the mouths of the women, sometimes two or three at a time, and humped there. When the first three came, flooding each pussy, they relaxed until their knots shrunk. When they withdrew they were immediately replaced by one of the second set. It was a scene from Dante's Inferno. Dogs ran everywhere, cum flying all over the women's bodies. Every dog moved to the women's mouths where their cocks were cleaned, sometimes pouring even more steaming cum directly into their bellies. This continued all night until the dogs were exhausted. Batman figured that each dog had cum four times, meaning each woman had been used twelve times,

Batman slapped the animal's rump. It reacted by surging forward driving its gargantuan cock into the waiting pussy. The animal started to hump. Each thrust drove the cock hard into Barbara's cervix. The pain was incredible, but even more incredible was the pleasure of its rubbing against her stretched pussy walls. No human pussy could hope to hold all the cum that donkey shot—☐uart after ☐uart after ☐uart. Semen poured from her cunt like water through a sieve. There was a huge puddle of the stuff on and beneath the bench. Eventually the cock shrunk and the donkey withdrew. Stephanie led the now docile animal back to its stall.

Batman told his slaves to clean themselves up and go home. He'd see to Barbara. Even unshackled she was unable to move. Batman blew his whistle and the well trained dogs returned to their kennels. Bruce Wayne's staff was mobilized via a call from the Batmobilephone. He did his best to dress Barbara but when he was finished everything was askew. He loaded her into the Batmobile and left just before the

crew came to remove the animals and break down the building. It would be stored in one of Wayne Enterprises' warehouses. Tomorrow nobody would be able to find any trace that the building even existed.

Batman parked the Batmobile, set the ICD, and led Barbara Gordon to her apartment. She leaked animal cum with every step. They met an older couple in the lobby who asked about Barbara's condition. "She's had a minor accident," he explained. They left satisfied. After all, if you couldn't trust Batman, who could you trust. Batman opened her door and took her right to the shower. He stood there naked, but for his cowl, and washed her thoroughly. He didn't really understand his actions; he wanted to destroy this woman. When he laid her into her bed she asked, "Do I know you? You know...your secret identy?"

Batman was taken aback. "Hard to say, maybe."

"One person I know you're not... is Bruce Wayne. He has a really small cock. I teased him mercilessly in high school. I've tried to apologize to him so many times but I've been too ashamed of my behavior. I don't know why I can tell you this, but after all I've been through ...." She fell asleep. Batman covered her and left, wondering what he should do next.

When he walked into his bedroom his slaves were there kneeling, naked and squeaky clean awaiting his pleasure.

CHAPTER 13

Bruce staggered into his bedroom at stately Wayne Manor and found his slaves waiting, eager to serve him. He gazed at their firm lush breasts that swayed as they breathed. "I need a shower,' he whispered. They rose to assist him with his clothes. Arm in arm they led him to the shower. While Marianne turned on the water Stephanie took the soap beginning to cleanse his aching shoulders and back. Between the two of them he was washed and dried in only moments. He was led to the bed where Stephanie massaged his manhood while Marianne rubbed his balls and fingered his ass. Despite his exhaustion he was soon rock hard and grown to maximum . Stephanie received only the slightest nod, a signal to continue. She straddled Bruce and gently lowered herself onto his shaft. The sensation was so intense that they both sighed simultaneously in rapture. Stephanie was an accomplished fuck-meister; she knew just how to encourage him. She initiated a slow rhythm and soon he followed. He reached up to a nipple and suckled. The other he rolled in his fingers,

pinched, and tugged. Their motions quickened; passions grew. Marianne could feel churning in his balls; Stephanie felt it in his cock. Bruce moaned, then grunted twice as Stephanie slid off the monster and slipped it into her mouth. Bruce felt that he had never cum so hard or so long. Stephanie did her best to swallow it all but was physically unable so Marianne licked up any scraps that dripped from her lips. Together they licked her secretions and any spare cum from his shrinking tool. He pulled them to him when they were done, slipped beneath the blankets, and they all fell quickly to sleep.

Bruce checked on all the dogs the following morning in the company of Stephanie. She was his secretary, after all. All the dogs who had mated with her recognized her scent and howled in their kennels as their penises extended from their sheathes. Precum was sprayed all over, but none reached either human. Once satisfied that the dogs had survived their ordeal Bruce returned to stately Wayne Manor. In the study he asked Stephanie, "I have tried everything to

humble and humiliate Barbara Gordon but nothing has worked. You're a woman. Any idea why?"

"Nothing you've done would have embarrassed me, but I'm a slut. I'll do anything. Maybe she is, too. I know she has a 'goody-two-shoes' reputation, but reputations aren't always accurate. Maybe she just needed something like this to realize what a whore slut she really is."

"Hmmm...maybe," he reflected. Later that day he saw Barbara at a Library meeting; they were both on the Council. He noticed she was hobbling. "Everything OK, Barbara? He inquired politely.

"Oh, just something that ran into me last night. I got a bit sore from it, but I'll be OK."

"Well, if you need any help...."

"Thank you, Bruce. Can I talk to you a moment? Bruce...Oh, I don't know how to start this. Bruce, something has happened to me lately that made me realize what a jerk I was in high school. I have tried to apologize for the way I treated you so many times, but, to be honest, I was ashamed of my behavior. Anyway, I want you to know how sorry I am. I hope you can forgive me." She walked away with tears in her eyes. Billionaire Bruce Wayne was dumbfounded. He just stood there with his mouth open until the meeting was called to order.

That night he snuck into Barbara's apartment again in his alter ego of Batman. It was late—after 11—but Barbara was waiting. She was wearing a wine red teddy made of fine lace except around her ample breasts which were fully exposed. A matching ribbon formed a triangle around each breast, extending to a bow at her neck supporting them. Not a word was spoken between them. She stepped forward leaned up and kissed him. Her lips parted as she pushed her tongue, wrestling with his between their mouths.

They had fucked, God knows how many times, in the past month; she had fucked dogs and a donkey; she had eaten a strange woman's ass, but this was their first kiss. Batman put his arms around her and pulled her to him in a tight embrace. His hands dropped to her ass. He gripped each cheek tightly as he ground his mammoth cock into her and she responded. When she broke the kiss she took his hand and led him to the bedroom. She helped him undress—everything but the cowl—and ran her hands over his body before settling them on his hard-on. He was fully erect now forcing her to stand slightly to one side lest she be skewered on it. She tried to drop to her knees but he pulled her up, supported her on his strong arms and lowered her slowly--cock meeting pussy perfectly. She had grown accustomed to his girth over the past weeks so she was able to accommodate him almost easily. He backed her up against the wall as he pushed her up and down on the Batprick. Idly, he wondered what the people next door would think of the noises, so obviously of active coupling. He fucked her hard, not to hurt or humiliate, but from his own passion. Everything he

gave her she returned, and then some. They came together sharing each other's spasms before collapsing into each other's arms. He carried her to the bed where they lay for some time.

She caressed his face, looking up into his eyes. "I did something today. I finally got up the nerve to apologize to Bruce Wayne. It was one of the hardest things I've ever done. I couldn't have done it without you."

"Me?" Batman asked.

"Yes," she said kissing him. "You helped me to grow out of that prudish shell I hated but wasn't strong enough to shed. Everything you forced me to do showed me just how strong I really am. That's what gave me the courage, and believe me I really needed it."

He rubbed her back and shoulders before pulling her down for a long deep kiss. It was a lovers kiss and they both knew it. When she backed off he asked, "So how did he take it?"

"I turned and walked away, but I could see him in a mirror. He just stood there with his mouth open. He didn't yell at me so I guess it was OK. I guess I'll find out soon enough."

Batman playfully fingered her butt. "I was wondering when you'd get to that," she said. "Got enough left to fuck me there. Damn, I want it so fucking badly. You know I never even dreamed of doing anal before you. Now I want it all the time." She rose and pushed her cunt down on the huge phallus to strengthen and moisten it; then repositioning, she guided it to her ass. All the recent ass-fucking had prepared her for this. She forced her anus open and her ass welcomed the intruder. Her rectum was slick and muscular, squeezing him tightly. He pushed himself through

her second sphincter so his cock was doubly constricted. Her friction made him hot and eager to cum. He started to gasp and pant. His actions became erratic. She rode him like a wild mustang until she milked him dry. She fell onto his chest, the cock still buried in her ass.

"You know," she began, "when this started I only did it because you were forcing me, blackmailing me. Are you forcing me now, blackmailing me now?"

"No, obviously not. You want me as much as I want you... maybe more, if possible."

She reached up and pulled him to another long kiss.

CHAPTER 14

Bruce didn't know what confused him more—her feelings or his? This wasn't what he anticipated. He wanted her to hate and fear him; he knew he hated her—or did he? He thought she was falling in love with him. He didn't love her—did he? It was all very confusing. Bruce maintained his normal daily activities, including all kinds of sex with his slaves, but his heart wasn't in it. He yearned for his nightly visits to Barbara. He loved her breasts with her long nipples—the longest he'd ever seen. He loved her huge clit, big enough to suck like a cock, and he did at every opportunity. He still remembered the first time he'd gone down on her. Her clit grew and when she got excited she arched her back jutting it out even farther. He licked her slit, savoring her flavor. He stuck his tongue deep into her wet cunt. She shivered in response. But when he started to suck her clit like a woman would suck his cock she went crazy.

She even squirted (ejaculated?) into his mouth. He loved it; so did she.

They fucked every night in every conceivable position. They did it standing up, sitting in a chair, leaning over the back of the couch, on the TV, on the kitchen counter. She sucked him off; she licked his ass and he did hers. Several times he brought a dog along and watched her couple with the beast. She grew accustomed to having the knot in her and having the dog flood her pussy so cum poured from her when the animal withdrew. She drank his cum, as well as everything the dog could give her. Batman gave her a golden shower, then squatted in the bath so she could pee all over him. They both loved the feeling of the hot pee running down their skin.

One day she asked him, "Will I ever get to see your face? You know who I am-- Barbara Gordon/Batgirl, but I don't know who you are. Don't you trust me?"

He had no answer for her but he wondered-- what brought that up? One day they met at the barn. Bruce's staff had erected it over the past two days. He brought her in and led her to the bench, but instead of restraining her, he laid on the bench himself, holding his wrists and ankles for her to shackle. It was his way of showing that he trusted her. She removed his Batman costume, but stopped when she got to the cowl. She had Batman powerless, under her total control, but her love and respect for him held her back. He'll show me when he's ready, she thought. She rubbed and teased his manhood. Soon he was fully in fuck mode. The cock was hard and hot; it twitched uncontrollably. She jerked it slowly, teasing him. She removed her clothing; Batman thought she had put on a little weight but it just made her look hotter. She straddled his head and lowered her snatch into his face. He licked it fanatically. He was hungry for her and it showed. He gnawed on her clit and pushed his tongue as deeply into her pussy as humanly possible. He used that tongue to fuck her, bringing her to her first orgasm. While she sat on his chest to recover

she stroked his stomach, noticing his fine-toned musculature. She turned and kissed him, something they had done more and more over the past few months. She moved into a reverse cowgirl fuck which showed her fine ass as it gyrated up and down his pole. When Batman was just about to cum she pulled off and squeezed the base of his cock, halting his ejaculation. Again she mounted him and when he got close she stopped it. Batman's balls were aching with the desire—the need—to cum. A third time she used the same trick. His cock throbbed in its need for release. Standing next to the bench she whispered, "See, I can be cruel, too. But you've suffered enough." She sat between Batman's legs facing him and wrapped her two hands around his rod. Slowly she started to stroke him. She increased the pressure of her fingers and moved her hands up and down faster and faster. Batman shook in his restraints until a huge river of semen flew three feet high before coming to rest on her face and mouth. All told he shot five times, soaking himself and her in sticky goo.

Batman was drained emotionally as well as physically from the huge orgasm. Barbara released him and

pulled him up to hug him, cum sticking between them. She licked cum from his face and chest. "Tell me, Batman, do you believe a child should know its parents?" He just looked at her, unsure of her meaning. "I'd like my child to know its father."

He smiled, reached back, and unzipped his cowl.

CHAPTER 15

Batman unzipped and loosened his cowl but didn't remove it. He pulled Barbara close and leaned down to kiss her. The cowl fell as their lips met. Both knew this was a special kiss; it was driven by more than passion or lust. When he broke the kiss he kept his face close to hers. He kissed and nibbled her earlobe and whispered, "I forgive you."

"Huh?" she replied, unsure of what he had spoken.

"I said, 'I accept your apology.'"

Barbara lurched back, seeing for the first time the face of her tormenter/lover. "Bruce?!!" She was speechless.

"Yep, it's me."

"But I don't understand. What happened to your...?"

"It's a long story. It happened when I...." She held her finger to his lips. "I've waited this long. I can wait a little longer--until you've given me more of what I need." She took his hand and led him back to the bench. What was supposed to be the site of her ultimate humiliation would become, instead, the site of her complete joy. She lay back on the bench. "Restrain me," she commanded him. "Then fuck me silly. Cum all over me. Then we'll talk."

Batman shackled her arms and feet. When she was secure he straddled her, forcing his cock down between her breasts. Holding them together he began a hot titty-fuck. When he lunged forward she licked and sucked on his tip, paying special attention to his pee hole. Bruce was getting hot again but he wanted to take care of his lover. He stood and backed up, lowering his cock over her cunt. He

pushed the shaft along her soaking slit. When his penis was wet he pointed it into her and pushed slightly. She raised her hips to welcome him. As he slid into her, making them one, they both moaned in the pleasure they were giving each other. They moved together, slowly at first, savoring every moment of their joining. Their pace increased until they were almost at doggie speed. Their wild humping had the predictable result—a rumbling from deep within began to control their very being. There was only one thing they cared for—to cum! It was only a matter of time. Barbara shook uncontrollably; Bruce's balls were afire. Then—THE ERUPTION! They shook violently and screamed in unison until they were, once again, in control of their bodies. Bruce sagged onto her chest, unshackling her arms just before he collapsed. She wrapped her arms around him.

He was still in her, still hard, when some minutes later she reached down to rub his balls. They felt hot, as if the fever of their sex was concentrated there.

"Undo my legs. I want you in my ass so I need to raise my legs." Bruce gladly complied. As he raised her legs he fingered her sphincter. It was wet with pussy juice that had leaked from their lovemaking. Barbara grabbed her ankles and pulled her legs up over her head. By doing so her asshole now pointed straight up, making easy access for the huge cock. He leaned down, pressing against her sphincter, forcing it open. An audible "POP" announced his entry. He proceeded slowly. He no longer wanted to hurt her. He pushed balls deep into her shitter. Looking into her face he saw an expression of euphoria-- of total rapture. He began his rhythm—in deeply, out to his head and then back in again. He fingered her pussy with one hand and rubbed her clit with the other. He brought her to heights she had never before attained—hell, never before even imagined. She bounced all over the bench, almost falling onto the floor several times. She came in an unending crescendo of orgasmic release. Just watching this forced Bruce's orgasm to the surface. It felt like his balls were clenched in a vise, so forcefully was the semen expelled from his body. It hit her

cervix with such force that, had she not been pregnant before she most certainly would be when he finished.

CHAPTER 16

They sat on the floor, his arm around her shoulders his hand caressing her breast, her hand lightly stroking him, keeping him semi-hard. He explained about his penis. "Yes, you were right when you teased me in high school. I had a tiny dick. Even erect it wasn't any bigger than your clit. But that all changed in a week's time. Junior year at Gotham Tech I studied in Europe and Asia. My research took me to Tibet. I had lost track of the time one day and couldn't find lodging, if there even was any, in this tiny Tibetan village. I wound up at the local monastery where the Lama took me in, fed me, and gave me a place to sleep. The next morning I went to

relieve myself at a slit trench the monks had dug as a toilet. I couldn't help but notice that every monk—every single one —had a huge organ. I think the smallest was about eight inches and that was soft. I asked the Lama about it and he told me about the secret process...and about the curse!"

"Curse?" she asked.

"Yes, I'll never forget his words, 'Whenever a woman sees or touches your organ she will have an uncontrollable urge to mate with you. That may seem a blessing, but many have found it is not. That is the curse.'"

"You don't really believe that stuff, do you?"

"Yes, I've seen it in action...many times. Even you told me you had an uncontrollable urge to touch and fuck it."

"Maybe," she said as she bent to kiss it, "but I think of it as a blessing. I love it."

"That's all part of the curse. I've witnessed it with many women, like my slaves.

"What? What do you mean...slaves?"

"Stephanie is both my secretary and my sex slave. She will do whatever I ask of her. I usually fuck her somewhere on her body every day. Also, I just took another, a 19-year old named Marianne. She used to be an upstairs maid at stately Wayne Manor. Now that we're together I'll get rid of them."

"Don't you dare!" she shouted. "Don't you think we can still make good use of them?"

"We? You mean you'd...."

"Sure," she said with a big smile crossing her face. "Didn't I love eating Stephanie's ass? I assume the other one is good looking."

"Not good looking—HOT! She's gorgeous and has a great body, too."

"I think I'm getting jealous. So what do they do for you?"

"They do everything, anything I ask."

"Hmmm. Would they do stuff with me?"

"If I asked them, of course. I set up that session in your apartment with Stephanie in advance and both girls knew all about the barn here."

"Do you pay them for all this?"

Bruce laughed. "Stephanie made 30 as my secretary. As my secretary/slave she makes 150. Marianne made 15 as a maid; now she makes 100. Does that answer your question?"

"Thousand? You pay Stephanie $150,000 to fuck you? That's incredible."

"She does more than that, they both do. They're on call 24/7. When you were getting dog and donkey fucked here in the barn I wasn't doing anything but watching. I got dirty, hot ,and really horny. When I got home they were there in my bedroom naked, kneeling, and all cleaned up—inside as well as out. They undressed me, ran me through the shower, and put me to bed. Of course, they fucked me silly before we all fell asleep. The agreement I have with

them...they can go anytime and I'll give them severance pay of 500 thousand to help them get started elsewhere. But they won't leave. They enjoy their work too much."

"Hmmm," Barbara thought as she snuggled into his chest.

Bruce gulped, almost afraid to ask. "Uh, have you been to the doctor?"

She looked at him and laughed. "Don't tell me the brave Batman is afraid of a little baby."

"No," he replied, "not afraid but maybe a little nervous."

"Yes, I went last week when I was over a month late. You must have poured a gallon of cum into me over

the past months so it's hardly surprising. I'm definitely pregnant although it's too early to tell the sex." She was smiling broadly when she finished, "I can't believe I'm going to be a mommy."

"Just call me Batdad," said Bruce, elated at the news.

CHAPTER 17

They continued to have wild sex every night—sometimes in her apartment, sometimes in the barn which was outfitted with a real bedroom—bed, lights, and a carpet—although they kept the bench for special fun and games.

Bruce was busy over the next several weeks managing his vast financial empire when he wasn't fighting crime. Twice Batgirl was involved in apprehending criminals. Batman chided her for risking the life of their child. Bruce decided there was only one way to dissuade her. He always attended the Gotham City Charity Ball, but at $500 a plate Batgirl

couldn't afford it. She didn't have his financial resources, not yet, anyway. He sent her a ticket, begging her to come. He had taken Stephanie in past years but now he wanted Barbara there.

Bruce could never tie the damned bow tie for his tux so he asked Stephanie for help. She adjusted it just before she said, "What's going to happen to me and Marianne?"

"What do you mean?"

I know you're really involved with Barbara Gordon. We're both happy for you but what about us?"

"You'll be happy to know that Barbara insists you stay. I think she has some ideas involving all of us. Good thing I have a big bed."

Stephanie looked relieved. She loved her Master but she was smart enough to realize she would never

advance beyond her status as a slave. She liked Barbara, too. Maybe it would be OK, after all.

Bruce left for the ball in his Bentley limo with his faithful butler Alfred at the wheel. Bruce preferred to drive himself so he never hired a chauffeur. On those occasions when he needed a driver Alfred was more than adequate. "We may have company on the way back, Alfred, at least I hope so."

"Miss Barbara, eh, sir?" It was impossible to fool Alfred.

Bruce had arranged the seating, much to the annoyance of the Ball's coordinator, but a $50,000 contribution had overcome his objections. All he really wanted was to be seated with Barbara Gordon and her father, Commissioner Gordon. He was at his seat when they arrived. He rose to greet them, Commissioner Gordon mistakenly thinking the salute was for him. Batman seated Barbara at his right with

the Commissioner on her other side. He made nervous small talk until virtually everyone was seated. The orchestra struck up their first number; Bruce took her hand and pulled her to the dance floor over her strenuous objections. "I'm not a good dancer," she complained.

"That's OK, I'm not planning to dance either." They were the only ones on the floor when Bruce went to one knee, kissed her hand and asked her, "Will you marry me?" Barbara turned red. She didn't know whether she should kiss him or kill him. Her mind raced; her head reeled. She couldn't believe that he actually wanted to marry—HER!—a policeman's daughter.

"Well?" his words brought her back to reality. "Everyone's watching and waiting for your answer." She looked around noticing that everyone was standing silently. Even the orchestra had stopped playing. She looked around some more, then at

Bruce. He was smiling and holding the biggest diamond ring she had ever seen. "YES!" she yelled. "YES! YES! YES!" Bruce rose, held her as he placed the ring on her finger, and looked into her eyes before entering into the best kiss either of them had ever experienced. The bystanders broke into applause. It wasn't every day that the world's most eligible bachelor decided to tie the knot. Friends rushed up to congratulate Commissioner Gordon. "I didn't even know they were seeing each other," displaying his usual keen sense of awareness.

Barbara did indeed accompany Bruce in the limo. "I'm very pleased Mr. Bruce decided to do right by you, especially after the brutal treatment he gave you for so long." Barbara looked at Bruce but he just shrugged his shoulders. He hadn't said a single word to the canny old butler.

They drove to Barbara's apartment where Bruce dismissed his faithful servant. "Tell the girls to go to bed. I'll see you in the morning."

"Oh, sure," Barbara chided him. "Get engaged to me and ruin my reputation all in a single night!" She was laughing so hard she could hardly stand. "I'm surprised my neighbors are even talking to me after all the noise we've made."

When they arrived at her door Bruce asked hesitatingly, "I want you to move into stately Wayne Manor where I know you'll be safe. Will you...please?"

"I will," she whispered as she initiated a long kiss," but I have one condition."

"What?"

"I'm not telling you, but you'll find out soon enough. Now let's go in and celebrate."

Bruce was shaking his head as they walked in, realizing at last that he would never fully understand any woman, let alone his future wife. They celebrated all night despite the frequent banging on the wall from Barbara's neighbors. But when they read the news in the morning paper even they were elated for the young couple. Although...they were overjoyed to learn that Barbara would be leaving the building. Maybe now they could get a decent night's sleep.

Bruce had his men pack up Barbara's clothing; her furniture, other than a few family heirlooms, was donated to charity. Barbara gave notice. No one blamed her. She had gone from a being a nobody to the future wife of one of the world's richest men. In a few weeks she was safely ensconced in stately Wayne Manor. Still Bruce had no idea what her condition might be. One night, after some particularly hard crime fighting he returned home and he was beat. He rose from the Reverse Bat Pole and then he

knew. Kneeling before him naked were the three women in his life. "May we serve...I mean, service you, Master," asked Barbara while the other two just smiled . Bruce nodded and pulled them up. Barbara leaned into him and whispered into his ear," Do you think we could have a dog?"

THE END

Made in the USA
Las Vegas, NV
22 March 2022